FOR JOOLS

(He's extremely
good at
sharing.)

And a special thank you to
Emily, Emma, Hannah,
Anna and Carolyn

First published 2015 by Macmillan Children's Books, a division of Macmillan Publishers Limited,
20 New Wharf Road, London N1 9RR.
Associated companies throughout the world www.panmacmillan.com
ISBN: 978-1-4472-7961-7 (HB)
ISBN: 978-1-4472-7962-4 (PB)
Text and illustrations © Zehra Hicks 2015. Moral rights asserted.
1 3 5 7 9 8 6 4 2
A CIP catalogue record for this book is available from the British Library.
Printed in China

ALL MINE!

Zehra Hicks

MACMILLAN CHILDREN'S BOOKS

It was lunchtime.

Mouse was just about to tuck
into a sandwich when . . .

ALL
MINE!

It's not nice to snatch. And it's bad manners to speak with your mouth full, you know.

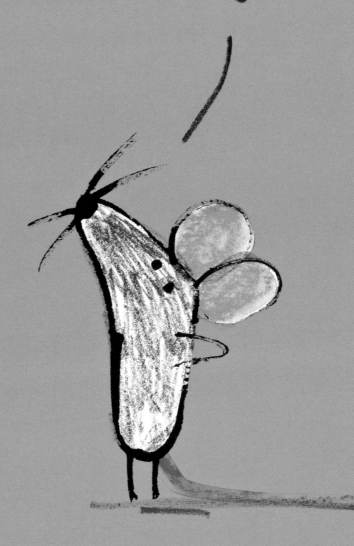

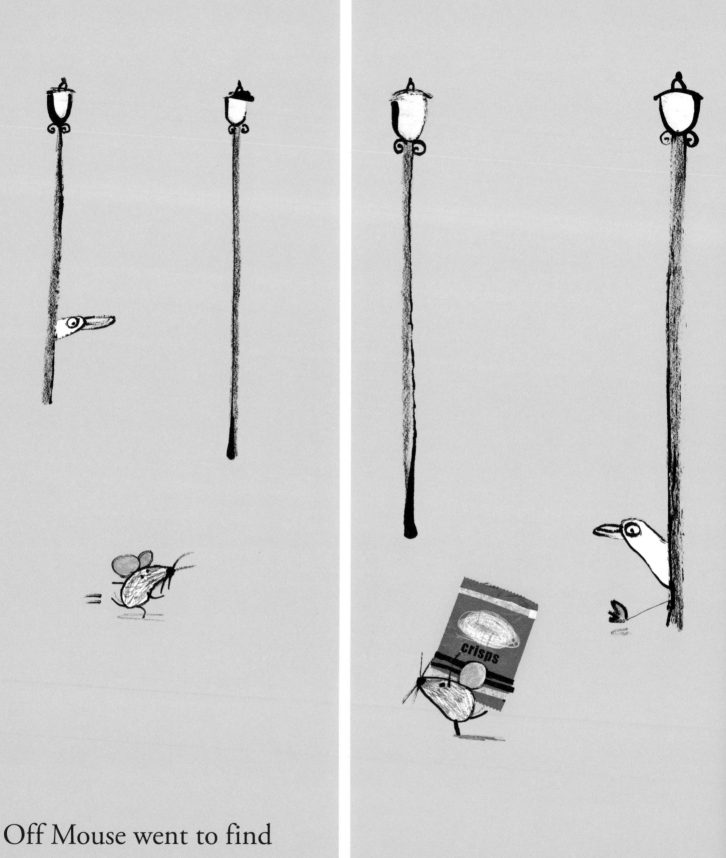

Off Mouse went to find
some more food.

Seagull followed.

You're very greedy and you're very rude. If you'd asked politely, perhaps I might have shared my crisps with you.

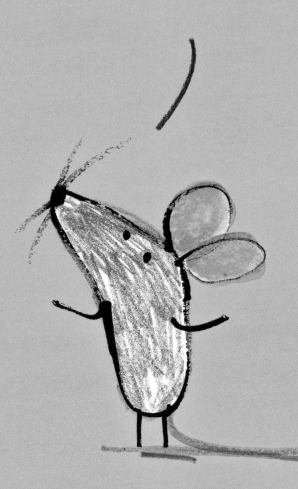

Mouse was still hungry.

So was Seagull.

CAKE!

MINE!
ALL ...

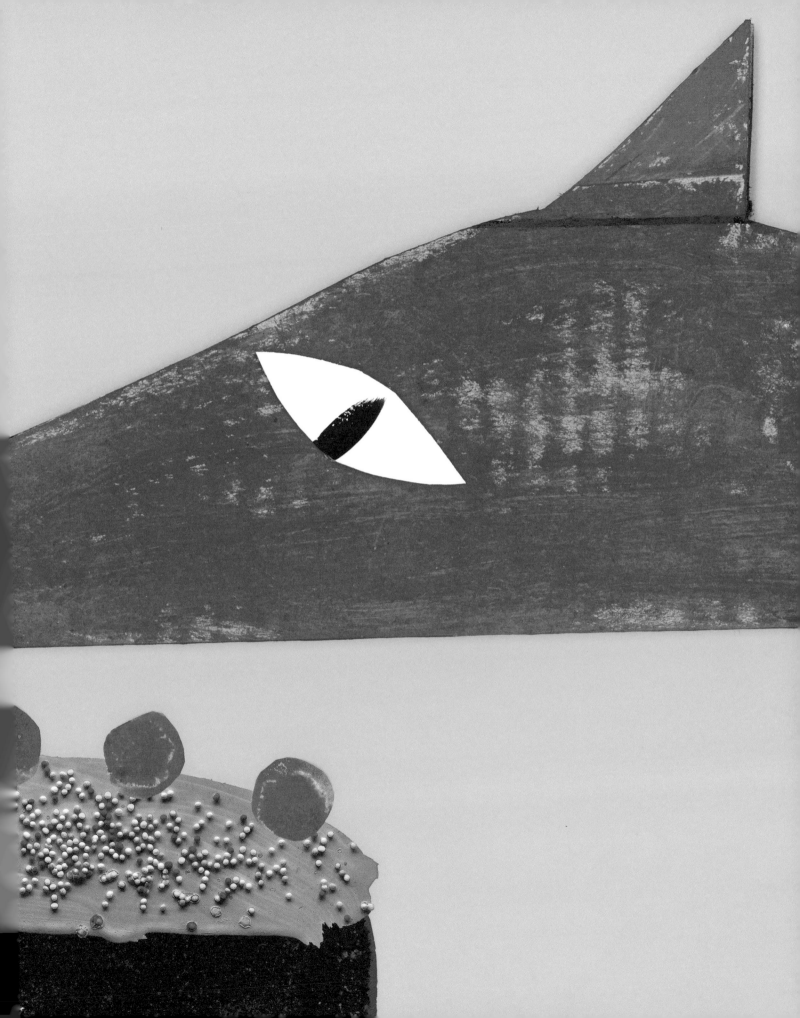

ANYONE FOR CAKE?

Awesome!

Yes,
please!

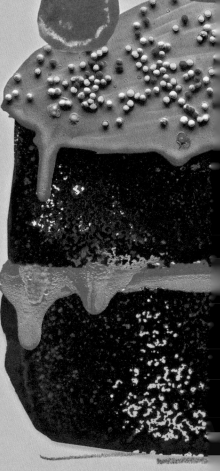